CALL ME AHNIGHITO

CALL ME AHNIGHITO

BY PAM CONRAD

PICTURES BY
RICHARD EGIELSKI

A LAURA GERINGER BOOK
An Imprint of HarperCollinsPublishers

For Paul Casey, who took me to the meteorite,
and Adrienne Betz, who remembered
—P.C.

Call Me Ahnighito
Text copyright © 1995 by Pam Conrad
Illustrations copyright © 1995 by Richard Egielski
Printed in the U.S.A. All rights reserved.

Library of Congress Cataloging-in-Publication Data
Conrad, Pam.
   Call me Ahnighito / by Pam Conrad ; pictures by Richard Egielski.
      p.   cm.
   "A Laura Geringer book."
   Summary: A huge meteorite describes how it lay half-buried in Greenland
for centuries until it was finally excavated by members of a Peary expedition.
   ISBN 0-06-023322-2. — ISBN 0-06-023323-0 (lib. bdg.)
   [1. Meteorites—Fiction.   2. Greenland—Fiction.   3. Peary, Robert E.
(Robert Edwin), 1856–1920—Fiction.]   I. Egielski, Richard, ill.   II. Title.
PZ7.C76476Cal   1995   93-5080
[E]—dc20   CIP
                                                                                  AC

Typography by Christine Kettner
1   2   3   4   5   6   7   8   9   10
❖
First Edition

AUTHOR'S NOTE

Call Me Ahnighito is the true story of the famous meteorite that sits in the American Museum of Natural History in New York City. The man who headed the discovery team in 1894 and finally brought Ahnighito (Ah-na-HEET-o) to New York in 1897 was Robert E. Peary, an adventurous man who was the first to reach the North Pole.

It was Peary's four-year-old daughter, along on the mission with her mother, who named the meteorite. According to some sources, this was the name of the native Greenlander who had cared for her as a baby.

When I was a child visiting the Planetarium and encountering Ahnighito for the first time, I imagined this gigantic piece of metallic rock hurtling through space. It is only as an adult that I have discovered the rest of the story.

But there is one part of the story that can still be told. When I was a teenager, I once visited Ahnighito with a friend. When the guard wasn't looking, my friend climbed on top of the giant meteorite and tucked a piece of paper into one of its small craters. The paper had our names on it. When I look at Ahnighito today, and in the mirror above, I wonder what the people who moved her to her current spot thought when they found that piece of paper. Did they wonder if our names had come from outer space? Probably not. Everybody knows that paper would have burned to dust shooting through space. But I *do* know that nobody has ever wondered what the meteorite was thinking—until now.   –P.C.

THEY CALL ME AHNIGHITO. And they tell me I am made of star stuff, but I don't remember my birth. I remember only the cold Arctic days when I sat for centuries, freezing cold and half buried in the hard and bitter earth. I sat and I waited, wishing that something, that anything would happen to me. But nothing did.

Nothing much ever happens in the Arctic. The Greenland sun comes up for a while, then sinks for a longer while. The ice begins to melt and then freezes again. For years and years, full of days and days, I saw nothing but the Greenland sky.

Then one day, the snow people came and gathered around me. I thought, *At last, something is happening.*

But they began to hammer at my sides and chip away little pieces of me. Imagine—little pieces of me! I worried that I would be chipped away to nothing.

Hundreds of melting summers passed and the snow people kept hammering away.

But soon they brought other people. These new people began to dig in the earth around my mighty sides. I thought they would chip away still bigger pieces of me, scattering me across the Arctic snows. Instead, they prodded and probed. Then, grunting and straining, they rolled me into the sun.

What joy I felt, free at last!

I hoped these new people would take me with them, away from the cold and the dark. But they were worried about the ice closing in on their boat, and they abandoned me.

I watched their ship sail south.

I thought I had been cold before. Now the wind blew across me and the snow touched places it had never touched before. I lay open, exposed and so alone.

I spent two long lonely winters wishing they would come back.

Then they returned. I watched them come sailing back into the bay. They sailed through the ice floes, coming back to get me, I was sure.

They began to work day and night with axes and picks and hydraulic jacks, banging and pounding, trying to lift me. They laid me on steel rails and thick timbers. Carefully, they rolled me along toward their ship, sweating and cursing all the while. They called me stubborn, obstinate, not knowing how I strained to help them.

Inch by inch, I went forward, pushed by jacks, pulled by chain blocks and steel cables, and crushing everything in my path. The rocks sparked beneath me as I flattened them. I bent the steel rails, and I shattered the timbers as the days grew colder and colder. They called me a monster as the snow began to swirl around them.

Then, with only inches to go—only inches, I tell you—a gale began, the winter's first blizzard, and they abandoned me once again.

Would they ever return?

I wept mightily as I watched them sail off without me. I never stopped looking for them. I *never* stopped.

And in time, when the sun was at its warmest, they came again, sailing toward me through a soggy snowstorm. I sat very still. Patiently, I waited.

They landed and built a bridge for me, a bridge of giant oak timbers spiked with iron rails. They greased the rails, steadied the ship, and then with mighty winches and groaning jacks, and with the tide exactly right so that the ship was at the perfect height, they tossed a flag across my back and began to shove me forward through the fog.

Inch by inch, they edged me across the gangplank. I dared not look down into the water. If the timbers had not held, if a wave had rocked the ship, I would have plunged into the bay and spent the rest of my days beneath the sea.

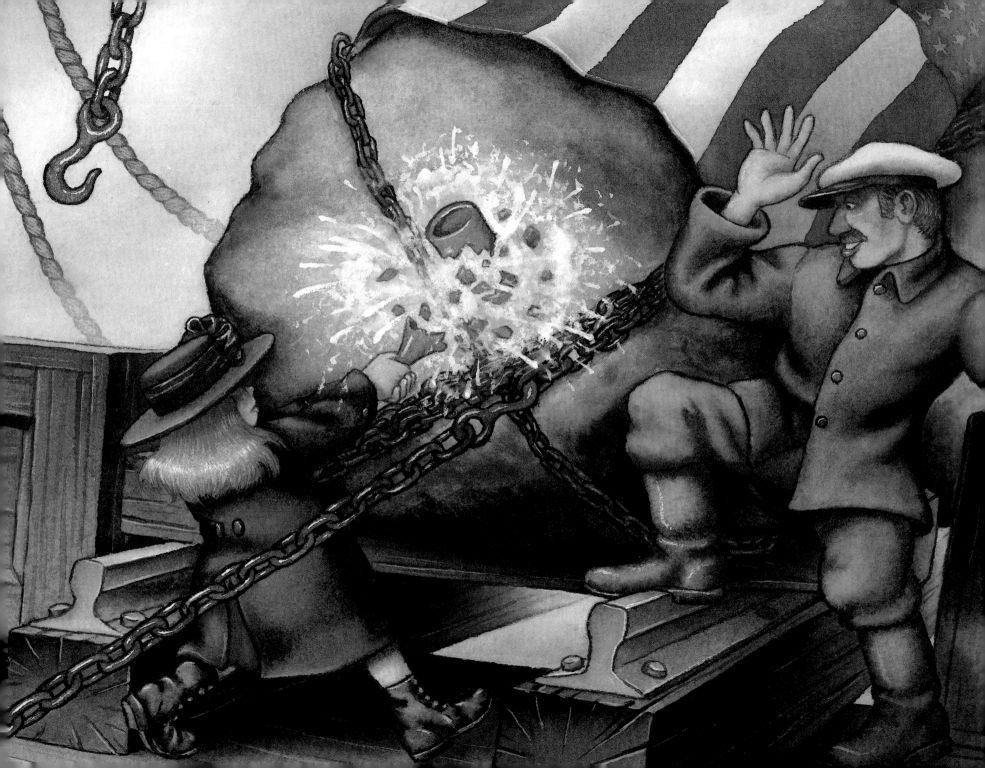

Suddenly a little child ran forward, and I froze in fear, waiting to see if we would topple into the water, but she broke a bottle against my side, and when the men laughed and cheered, she called out, "I name you Ahnighito!"

At that instant the sun broke through the fog, showing sky patches of blue, and the sun streaked from its low midnight place and lit me like a jewel.

Ahnighito.

They pushed me the rest of the way and eased me into the ship's hold. My bulk settled into the ship. *Ahnighito*, I thought. *A most wonderful name.*

For days I heard the ship plowing into icebergs and bashing into floating ice floes, trying to cut her way out of the bay into the open sea.

Once at sea, the men were upset with me because all the ship's compasses pointed at me and at nothing else. I listened to the Arctic waves and savage wind beat at the creaking ship. It was a long and troubling journey.

In nearly a month's time, we were in a warmer place, a bright place. The men tied up to a busy dock, and with the help of a giant crane and a sling of thick chains, I was lifted from the deep hold of the ship and laid out in the sun.

Soon I learned I was in the Brooklyn Navy Yard. Everyone who passed wondered what on earth I was.

"What's this rock doing here?" they would ask.

Call me Ahnighito, I thought. *I am Ahnighito.*

But, of course, no one knew.

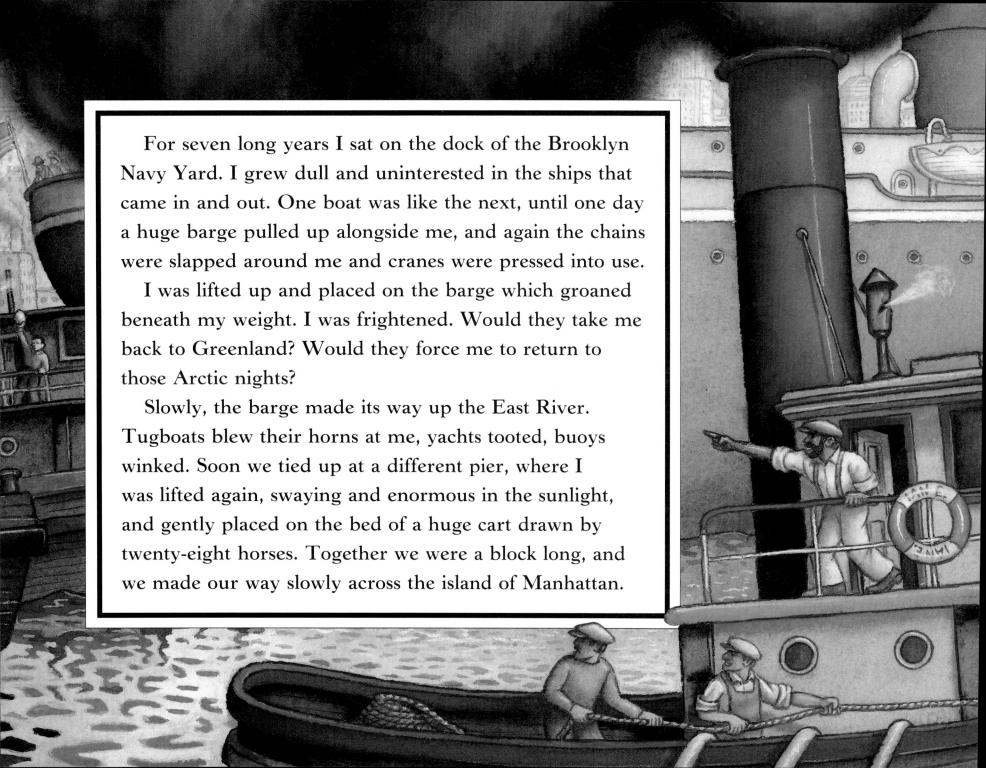

For seven long years I sat on the dock of the Brooklyn Navy Yard. I grew dull and uninterested in the ships that came in and out. One boat was like the next, until one day a huge barge pulled up alongside me, and again the chains were slapped around me and cranes were pressed into use.

I was lifted up and placed on the barge which groaned beneath my weight. I was frightened. Would they take me back to Greenland? Would they force me to return to those Arctic nights?

Slowly, the barge made its way up the East River. Tugboats blew their horns at me, yachts tooted, buoys winked. Soon we tied up at a different pier, where I was lifted again, swaying and enormous in the sunlight, and gently placed on the bed of a huge cart drawn by twenty-eight horses. Together we were a block long, and we made our way slowly across the island of Manhattan.

Children ran beside us, trying to touch me. Men held on to their derbies, women waved their gloves. It was a most splendid procession. And at the end, I found my home.

Now I am at my most glorious. I am displayed in the center of a warm room with mirrors above me so that people can admire me from all sides. And there are signs telling all about me so that I can be understood.

I am no longer lonely. Everyone knows my name. They call me Ahnighito.

It's a good life, being a famous old meteorite. Sometimes, late at night, when the bright lights are dimmed and the guard has gone home, I bask in the soft warmth of the museum and think about my life.

I even think sometimes that maybe, if I were to try very hard, I might remember my birth, and how I was made of star stuff.